Donald Crews
Parade

A MULBERRY PAPERBACK BOOK • New York

For all of you
I always remember
and for any of you
I sometimes forget

Library of Congress Cataloging in Publication Data
Crews, Donald. Parade.
Summary: Illustrations and brief text present the various elements of a parade—the spectators, street vendors, marchers, bands, floats, and the cleanup afterwards.
1. Parades—Juvenile literature.
[1. Parades—Pictorial works] I. Title.
GT3980.C73   1983   394′.5   82-20927
ISBN 0-688-06520-1

First Mulberry Edition, 1986

NO PARADE TODAY PARKING

Buttons, balloons, and flags for sale.

Hot dogs, pretzels, ice cream, and soda to buy.

ICE CREAM

CANDY

SODA

Watchers
gather.

ICE CREAM

CANDY

SODA

A crowd. **Waiting.**

Here it
comes!

Flags
flying.

A strutting
drum major
leads the
marching band.

cornets,

trumpets, flutes,

French horns   **sousaphones,**

field drums, cymbals, and last the big bass drums.

Here comes
a float,

and baton twirlers, twirling and turning.

Bicycles from bygone days,

a cruise ship,

and at the end
of the parade,
the brand-new
fire engine.

Nothing left
to see,
nothing left
to do except . . .